THE GATOR GIRLS

GET WELL, GATORS!

by **Stephanie Calmenson**
and **Joanna Cole**

illustrated by
Lynn Munsinger

Morrow Junior Books
New York

Pen-and-ink with watercolor was used for the full-color illustrations.
The text type is 18-point Palatino.

Published by Morrow Junior Books
a division of William Morrow and Company, Inc.
1350 Avenue of the Americas, New York, NY 10019
www.williammorrow.com

Printed in the United States of America.

2   3   4   5   6   7   8   9   10

Library of Congress Cataloging-in-Publication Data
Calmenson, Stephanie.
Get well, gators!/by Stephanie Calmenson and Joanna Cole;
illustrated by Lynn Munsinger.
Summary: When Allie Gator comes down with swamp flu,
she worries that she will miss the street fair being held in her neighborhood.
ISBN 0-688-14786-0 (trade)—ISBN 0-688-14787-9 (library)
[1. Alligators—Fiction.   2. Sick—Fiction.   3. Fairs—Fiction.]   I. Cole, Joanna.   II. Munsinger,
Lynn, ill.   III. Title.   IV. Series: Calmenson, Stephanie. Gator Girls.
PZ7.C136Ge 1998   [Fic]—dc21   97-15756   CIP   AC

CONTENTS

1
FRONT-PAGE NEWS!

Ring! Ring! Early one morning the telephone rang at Allie Gator's house. Allie was still half-asleep when she picked up the phone.

"Hullo," she mumbled.

"Hi, it's me—Amy," said Amy Gator.

Allie already knew it was Amy. Allie and Amy were best friends. When they were not together, they were talking on the phone.

"What's up?" Allie yawned.

"I am, but you're not!" said Amy.

"Very funny," said Allie.

"Let's go to the playground," said Amy. "I'll give you five minutes to get ready and one to get downstairs."

"See you in six," said Allie, putting on her glasses. She was wide awake now.

Allie and Amy lived in apartment buildings next door to each other. They each lived on the sixth floor.

At the same time, they got into their elevators. They each pressed the first floor button, then watched the numbers light up. *Six, five, four, three, two, one!*

The Gator Girls burst out of their doors at the exact same time.

"We're amazing!" said Amy.

"You can say that again," said Allie.

"We're amazing!" said Amy.

"Very funny," said Allie. "I'll race you to the playground."

It was a heads-and-tails tie all the way. When they got there, they came to a screeching stop. The playground was shut tight, with a big lock on the gate. A sign read:

CLOSED
UNTIL
FURTHER
NOTICE

"Closed?" said Allie. "What are we supposed to do without a playground?"

"It's too horrible even to think about!" said Amy.

"Come on," said Allie. "We might as well go home."

The Gator Girls did an about-face. On the way back, they passed a newsstand and saw a copy of the *Swamp Town Reporter.*

"Look! Front-page news!" said Allie.

The headline read:

TOWN PLAYGROUND NOT SAFE!

The Gator Girls stopped to read all about it.

2
THE MOST
OBNOXIOUS GATORS

The report in the paper said the town needed new playground equipment.

"'The town will be holding a street fair to raise money,'" read Allie. "Wow! That means games and rides and food."

"We can have a booth," said Amy.

"Let's do something new and different," said Allie.

"I know! We could have a storytelling booth," said Amy. "We're good at that."

Just then a bouncy, bubbly alligator came along. She had braces on her teeth and a T-shirt with her name on it. It was Gracie! She always made the Gator Girls laugh.

"Hi!" said Gracie. "Did you hear about the fair? We should have a joke-telling booth. I already have a great joke. What did the Ferris wheel say to the carousel?"

"We give up," said Amy.

"See you around...and around...and around!" said Gracie.

The Gator Girls rolled their eyes.

"We were thinking about a storytelling booth," said Allie.

"Ooh, that's a good one," said Gracie. "It can be an Instant Story Booth."

"Cool," said Amy. "Whoever buys a ticket will tell us three facts about themselves. Then we'll make up a fabulous story on the spot."

"Let's try it. Here are three facts about me," said Allie. "One: I am green. Two: I wear glasses. Three: I had trouble waking up this morning. In fact, I'm still kind of tired."

"Stay awake for your story," said Amy. "Once upon a time there was a green alligator who took her glasses off at night when she went to sleep."

Gracie continued the story.

"In the morning the alligator had trouble getting up. The window shades were down, so she could not see the sun. Her glasses were off, so she could not see the clock."

"She did not know it was time to get up," said Allie, picking up where Gracie left off. "The alligator slept for forty days and forty nights. Finally..."

Whoosh! Something almost knocked

Allie off her feet. That something was...

"MARVIN!!! Why don't you watch where you're going!" called Allie.

"Why don't you watch where you're standing!" Marvin answered.

Marvin was the most obnoxious alligator ever.

Whoosh! Something else missed Amy's toes by a gator nose.

"DAVE!!!" yelled Amy.

Dave was the new gator in town. He was the second most obnoxious alligator ever.

"You're blocking traffic," said Dave. "You could get a ticket for that."

"Speaking of tickets," said Allie, "we'll be *selling* them at our booth."

"What? The Goony Gators' Booth?" asked Marvin.

"That's so funny I forgot to laugh," said Amy. "For your information, we're having an Instant Story Booth."

"That's so boring, I forgot to wake up," said Dave.

"We're giving skateboard lessons at our booth," said Marvin.

"Oh, really? Then we'd better have a Band-Aid Booth," said Gracie.

"Just for that, we're going to charge you double," said Marvin.

"You are so obnoxious. We wouldn't go

to your booth even for free," said Allie.

"Come on," said Amy. "We don't have time to waste."

"That's right," said Allie. "We have places to go!"

"Things to do!" said Amy.

"Gators to see!" said Gracie.

The three gators linked arms, put their noses in the air, and stomped off. The truth was, they had no idea where they were going.

3
WHAT'S THE MATTER WITH ALLIE?

"There's the candy store," said Gracie. "Let's get some Gooby Gumbos."

They filed into the store. Jasmine, the owner, was juggling bags of candy.

"Hi," said Allie. "What are you doing?"

"I'm practicing my act for the talent show at the street fair," said Jasmine.

"Wow! A talent show!" said Allie.

The gators bought three bags of candy and went outside.

"I'll be a stand-up comic," said Gracie. "I'm going home to make up some jokes." She waved and ran off.

"What should *we* do in the show?" Amy asked Allie after Gracie left.

Allie didn't answer. She was in the middle of a yawn.

"We could tap dance," said Amy.

"No tapping now," said Allie. "My head hurts." She started to open her Gooby Gumbo bag.

"We can sing, too. We'll do a duet," said Amy, ignoring Allie's complaint. Amy started to make up a song.

One-a-croc, two-a-croc,
Three-a-croc, rock!
Who's at the door?
Listen, knock knock!
I'm Amy!

She turned to Allie.

"Come on—it's your turn," said Amy. "You have to sing 'I'm Allie.'"

"No singing now," said Allie. "I told you, my head hurts."

Allie was still trying to open her bag of candy. Amy continued the song alone.

I'm Amy! That's Allie.
Let us in and we'll begin.
We'll sing and dance
and jump and spin!

Amy started jumping and spinning. Allie did not join her. She was trying to tear her candy bag with her teeth. *Rippp!* It split wide open. Gooby Gumbos flew out of the bag and rolled all over the street.

Allie stomped her foot. "Look what you made me do!" she cried.

"I didn't make you do anything," said Amy. "You're such a grump. It's only candy."

"That's easy for you to say. You've got a whole bag of it," said Allie.

"Here, have some of mine," said Amy.

She opened her bag without any trouble and shook some candy into Allie's hand.

Allie stuffed the handful of Gooby Gumbos into her mouth. *"Ptooey!"* She spit them all out.

"Gross!" she said.

"What's the matter now?" asked Amy.

"There was a blue one," said Allie. "I *hate* blue ones."

"I can't believe you!" said Amy. "You never hated blue Gooby Gumbos before."

"Well, I hate them now," said Allie. "And if you like them so much, *you* eat them," said Allie. "I'm going home."

Allie spun on her heels and disappeared down the street. Amy sat on a bench and began to eat her Gooby Gumbos.

Allie's so grouchy, she thought, eating a green one.

She won't sing or dance, thought Amy, eating a red one.

And she spit out perfectly good Gooby Gumbos, thought Amy, popping a blue one into her mouth.

I wonder what's the matter with Allie, thought Amy. The blue ones taste perfectly good to me.

4
SWAMP FLU

Allie trudged in through her door. Her father took one look at her and asked, "Do you feel okay?"

Allie's mother felt her forehead.

"My goodness! You have a fever. You're going right to bed," she said.

While Allie's mother tucked her in, her father called Dr. Bogwell.

In no time the doorbell was ringing. Dr. Bogwell rushed into Allie's room. He had a stethoscope around his neck and a big smile across his face.

"Aha! Here's my patient!" he said. "Now, where's my tongue depressor?" He reached into his bag and pulled out a soup ladle. "No, that's not it," he muttered. He pulled out a rubber chicken. "No, that's not it," he said. Finally he found what he was looking for.

"Please stick out your tongue and say 'ahh,'" said Dr. Bogwell. He held the tongue depressor out to Allie's father.

"Oops! Wrong patient," said Dr. Bogwell.

He turned to Allie. Allie stuck out her tongue.

"Blahhh!" she said grumpily.

"Hmm. Let me check your ears," said Dr. Bogwell. "Where's my flashlight?"

He reached into his bag again. He pulled out a tuna sandwich.

"Nope," he said. He pulled out a deck of cards. "Guess not," he said. Finally Allie heard him say, "Ah, yes, here it is."

He shined the light into Allie's ear.

"Amazing! I can see all the way through to the other side," said Dr. Bogwell.

Allie groaned. She felt too sick to laugh.

Dr. Bogwell stuck a thermometer in

Allie's mouth. He studied the pink spots popping up on her cheeks.

"Tell me, how are you feeling?" he asked.

Allie tried to talk with the thermometer in her mouth.

"Murgle, shmurgle, murgurh," she said.

"Oh, my. This is more serious than I thought," said Dr. Bogwell, pulling out the thermometer. "She can't even talk!"

"What's she got, doctor?" asked Allie's father nervously.

"She's got a purple tongue, her temperature's red hot, and she's starting to get pink spots," said Dr. Bogwell. "It's a classic case of swamp flu!"

"What can we do for her?" asked Allie's mother.

"She must have one full week of bed rest," said the doctor.

"One week? No way! I'll miss the street fair!" cried Allie.

"She'll need one full bowl of peat moss soup every day," continued Dr. Bogwell.

"Peat moss soup? You can't mean it!" croaked Allie.

"Also a dressing of wet marsh hay on her spots every three hours," said the doctor.

"Wet marsh hay? That's the last straw!" said Allie.

She snapped the covers up over her head. In no time she was fast asleep.

When Allie woke up, the doctor was gone and her father was talking on the phone.

"I'm sorry, Amy," he said. "Allie's asleep."

"I'm not sleeping," said Allie weakly. "Please let me talk."

Allie's father handed her the phone.

"Hi, Amy," said Allie. "Guess what? I have swamp flu."

"So that's why you were grumpy," said Amy.

"I have to stay in bed a whole week," said Allie. "I can't even go to the fair."

"Oh, no! What about our song?" said Amy.

"You'll have to sing it by yourself," said Allie.

"I can't sing in front of the whole town by myself! I'm too scared," said Amy.

There was silence at the other end of the phone.

"Allie, did you hear me?" asked Amy. "Allie? Allie?"

Allie's mother came on the line. "Allie fell asleep, Amy," she whispered. "She'll have to talk to you later."

As soon as Amy hung up the phone, she felt lost. She was salt without pepper. She was a bat without a ball. She was Amy without Allie! What was she going to do?

Then Amy had an idea.

5
GREETINGS,
FORTUNE-SEEKER

Amy grabbed a handful of dimes and went to Madame Lulu's Fortune-Telling Parlor. It was pink and yellow outside but dark and gloomy inside. It was always a little scary going in. Amy stood frozen to the spot.

"Are you there, Madame Lulu? I need you," called Amy from the front step.

"Greetings, fortune-seeker," said Madame Lulu. "Come in."

Amy inched her way inside. Soon she was face-to-face with Madame Lulu.

Madame Lulu wore a black veil on her head. She had about twenty bracelets on each arm. The bracelets clinked whenever she moved.

Madame Lulu held out her hand. *Clink!*

Amy put a dime in Madame Lulu's palm. Madame Lulu dropped it into her pocket. *Clink!*

"Tell me, where is the friend who always comes with you?" asked Madame Lulu.

"Allie has swamp flu," said Amy.

"Swamp flu!" cried Madame Lulu. She gazed into her crystal ball. "It says she'll get better soon. Thank goodness."

"But she has to stay in bed all week," said Amy. "And we were supposed to do a duet at the talent show."

"I guess you'll be doing a solo now," said Madame Lulu, grinning.

"It's no joke," said Amy. "Without Allie, anything could happen. I might get a swamp toad in my throat!"

"Let me check my crystal ball," said Madame Lulu.

She pressed her face up close and squinted into the glass dome.

"I see words. But I can't read them.

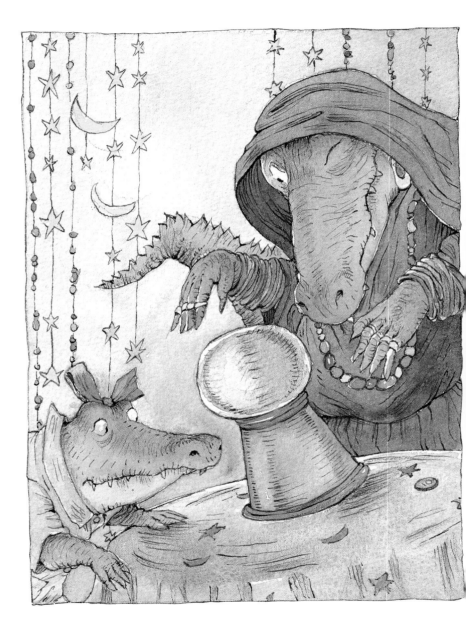

They're too fuzzy," said Madame Lulu, holding out her palm. *Clink!*

Amy handed Madame Lulu another dime.

"Ah, much better!" said Madame Lulu, going into a trance. "The crystal ball is puzzled. Have you ever had swamp toads before?"

"Well, no," said Amy. "I haven't."

"And I heard you gave a great school report last month," said Madame Lulu.

"That's right," said Amy.

"And you did it by yourself in front of your whole class," said Madame Lulu.

"I did pretty well, too," said Amy proudly.

"Then I'm sure you'll do fine in the talent show," said Madame Lulu. "Wait! Hold everything! The crystal ball is interrupting us for an important message."

Madame Lulu peered into the ball again.

"It says: *The show must go on!*" she said.

"Of course! We need money for the playground," said Amy. "Thank you, Madame Lulu! Thank you!"

6
GROSS-OUT!

Amy ran outside and used one of her dimes to call Allie from a pay phone.

"Hi, Allie! I couldn't wait to talk to you. I'm calling from outside!" she shouted. "I just saw Madame Lulu and she said I'll do fine singing a solo. Now all we need to do is finish writing our song."

Amy heard Allie's mother talking in the background.

"Finish your peat moss soup, dear," she said. "Then you can talk."

Amy could not see Allie holding her nose and making yucky faces, but she could hear her slurping noisily. She held the phone away from her ear. It knocked right into...

"MARVIN!!!" cried Amy.

Marvin wobbled wildly on his skateboard.

"Hey, watch that phone!" he said.

Dave peeked around the corner.

"Don't tell me you're all alone, Amy. Where's Allie?" he asked.

"I'm here," came Allie's voice from the phone.

"In the telephone? That's too goony even for you," said Dave.

"For your information, Mr. Know-It-All, I'm home sick with swamp flu," said Allie. She had finally finished her soup.

The next thing they heard was Allie shrieking, "No, Mom! Not wet marsh hay!"

"Hey, hey, what did you say?" said Marvin, laughing. "Get it? Hey? Hay?"

"Very funny," said Allie. "But I don't have time to talk to silly gators. I have important medical treatments to attend to."

"I'll call you later so we can write the song," said Amy, hanging up.

"What song?" asked Marvin.

"The one I'm singing in the talent show," said Amy. "What are you doing?"

"We have a great act," said Marvin. "We're doing our imitation of seasick gorillas."

Before Amy could stop them, Marvin and Dave started beating their chests and making disgusting sounds.

"How's *that* for talent?" asked Dave.

"Talent? I don't think so!" said Amy.

"Well, if you don't like that, we can do our imitation of centipedes getting stepped on," said Marvin.

Marvin and Dave fell down on the ground and inched forward a few steps.

They took turns moaning, *"Splat! Gurgle! Squish!"*

"Yuck! What a gross-out!" said Amy. "You gators are too revolting even to think about!"

Before Marvin and Dave could answer, Amy turned around and stomped off with her nose in the air. She went straight home and dialed Allie's number.

7
LISTEN TO THIS!

Bzzz, bzzz, bzzz, bzzz, bzzz....

Allie's line was busy. Amy tried again and again, but she could not get through.

I guess Allie will call me later, thought Amy. I'll start working on the song by myself.

She went to her room and closed the door. She began to sing.

One-a-croc, two-a-croc,
Three-a-croc, rock!
Who's at the door?
Listen, knock knock!
I'm Amy!

Amy stopped. It was Allie's turn to say, "I'm Allie."

Uh-oh. I'll have to skip that, thought Amy. She kept singing.

Let us in and we'll begin...

"I can't say *us*!" cried Amy. "It's only *me*."

Amy knew the song was no good. She had to make up a song she could sing by herself. She thought and thought.

Amy picked up a hairbrush. She held it to her mouth like a microphone. But she needed an audience. Amy looked around her room.

"Goldie!" she said to her goldfish. "Listen to this!"

I'm Amy Alligator,
And I'm here all alone.
We need money for our playground
So I'm singin' on my own.

Goldie flipped her tail in her bowl. Amy smiled and went on singing.

We need brand-new swings
And monkey rings.
We need...
Ring! Ring!
A telephone?

No, wait. That's *my* telephone, thought Amy. She answered it.

"Hi, are you ready to write the song?" asked Allie.

"Ready? I already finished it!" said Amy.

"You did? Without me?" said Allie.

Amy was too excited about her song to hear the disappointment in Allie's voice.

"It's good, too. My goldfish loves it," Amy exclaimed.

She sang the song from start to finish. With each new line, Allie felt more left out. The song was all about Amy and the playground. There was not a word in it about Allie.

"Nice song...for a fish," mumbled Allie. "I have to go now. I'm a very sick alligator, and I need my rest. Doctor's orders."

"Okay," said Amy. "While you're resting, I'll write another song."

"You do that," said Allie, plunking down the phone.

Amy went to work on her new song. When she finished, she said to Goldie, "Now for great song number two!"

Amy moved to the mirror so she could watch herself sing. Then she picked up her hairbrush and sang her new song all the way through.

Goldie flipped her tail, and Amy took a bow.

"Get ready, Swamp Town!" she said. "I'm going to be a star!"

8
STARS OF
THE SHOW

On the morning of the fair, Allie heard everyone getting ready outside. She went to the window and looked down.

Madame Lulu was carrying her crystal ball into her fortune-telling booth. Marvin and Dave were hanging up their Skateboard Lessons sign. Amy and Gracie were watching some gators building a stage for the talent show.

"Hi, Amy! Hi, Gracie!" Allie called out the window. "I'm over here!"

But there was so much noise that her friends didn't hear her.

When the stage was finished, Madame Lulu stepped up to the microphone.

"Gather round, fair-goers!" announced Madame Lulu. "My crystal ball says a great show is about to begin."

The audience rushed to the stage while the performers got ready. Allie saw Amy put on a sparkly ribbon and bright red tap shoes.

Amy gets to be a star. All I get to be is sick, thought Allie. Everyone's forgotten me.

She looked at her old bathrobe and fuzzy slippers. There wasn't a sparkle in sight. How depressing! Allie trudged back to bed and pulled the covers over her head. Soon she was asleep.

The talent show went on without her. The audience was grossed out when Marvin and Dave did their imitations. They laughed when Gracie told her jokes. And they swayed along with the music when Dr. Bogwell and Madame Lulu danced a waltz.

Then it was Amy's turn. There was a big round of applause as she went on stage. She looked up at Allie's window. She wished Allie were there to cheer her on.

"Ahem! Ahem!" Amy cleared her throat. No swamp toads were present. Amy was ready. She had two great songs, and she wanted everyone to hear them—especially Allie.

Amy snapped her fingers and tapped her tail. Then she began to sing.

I'm Amy Alligator
And I'm here all alone.
We need money for our playground
So I'm singin' on my own.

When Amy finished her song, the audience cheered. She looked up at Allie's window. Allie still wasn't there. But Amy had to go on.

"This next song is dedicated to my best friend, Allie," she said. Then she sang:

Allie Gator, lose your spots.
I sure miss you lots and lots.

While Amy was singing, Allie was tossing and turning in her bed. She dreamed that she was all alone and lost in a strange place. Would anyone come to find her? Suddenly in her dream she heard someone calling her name.

Allie Gator! I miss you!
Allie Gator! No more flu!

Allie smiled and opened her eyes. She was awake now, but she could still hear the voice from her dream. It was Amy's voice calling, "Everybody sing along!"

Allie jumped out of bed and headed for the window. The next thing Allie knew, the whole town was waving to her and singing:

Allie Gator! Get well quick!
Allie Gator! Don't be sick!

Allie waved back. She wasn't wearing tap shoes or a sparkly bow. But thanks to her friend Amy, she felt like a star.

9
GET YOUR INSTANT STORY HERE!

When Amy's performance was over, she and Gracie moved the Instant Story Booth below Allie's window.

"Now you can be part of the booth," called Amy.

"This is so great," said Allie.

"Get your instant stories here!" called Gracie. "Don't be shy! Step right up!"

A moment later, two customers appeared. They were…

"MARVIN!!!" called Allie from the window.

"DAVE!!!" said Amy from the street.

"We want a story about the two of us," said Marvin, handing over two tickets.

"Here are three facts," said Dave. "First, we're the coolest gator guys on the block."

"Second," said Marvin, "we're the coolest gator guys in town."

"Third, we're the coolest gator guys in the country!" said Dave.

"We should have known you'd be obnoxious," said Allie, rolling her eyes. "Okay, here's your story: Once upon a time there were two gator guys. They thought they were the coolest ever."

Amy continued, "They were cooler than wind. They were cooler than snow."

"They were so cool someone thought they were ice cubes and dropped them

into a pitcher of lemonade," said Gracie, flapping her arms.

"Those cool gator guys melted away to nothing," called Allie. "And that is...

"*The end!*" shouted Amy, Allie, and Gracie together.

"Did you say 'the end'?" said Dave.

"That's the best news we've heard yet," said Marvin.

Amy yawned.

"Are we boring you?" asked Marvin.

"No more than usual," said Amy grumpily.

"What's the matter?" asked Gracie.

"I feel kind of funny," said Amy.

"You look funny, too," said Marvin. "You're starting to get polka dots!"

Amy looked down. Pink spots were coming out all over her.

"Oh, no! I've got swamp flu!" she cried. "I'd better go home right away!"

10
GET WELL, GATORS!

Ring! Ring! A few hours later, the telephone rang at Amy's house. It was Allie.

"How are you?" asked Allie.

"Terrible," said Amy. "I have to stay in bed one full week, eat one full bowl of—"

"I know. Peat moss soup," said Allie. "Isn't it awful?"

Amy did not answer.

"Amy? Are you there?" said Allie.

There was silence at the other end. Amy was fast asleep.

A few days later, Amy felt better and called Gracie.

"Dr. Bogwell just left," Gracie said. "My mother's making me peat moss soup."

"Oh, no!" cried Amy. "Swamp flu!"

When Gracie was a little better, she called Marvin.

"I can't talk now," said Marvin. "I'm getting a wet marsh hay dressing."

"Hey, hey, what did you say?" joked Gracie. "You've got swamp flu, too!"

When Marvin was better, he called Dave.

"I see spots!" yelped Dave.

"Where?" asked Marvin.

"All over me," groaned Dave.

"Welcome to the Swamp Flu Club," said Marvin.

Thirty-five bowls of peat moss soup, two hundred wet marsh hay dressings, and four hundred pink spots later, all five gators were well again—just in time for the opening of the new playground. The gators burst out their doors.

"Hey, hey, we're okay!" called Marvin.

"Please, no more hay!" joked Gracie.

"And no more soup!" said Allie.

"Or spots!" said Amy.

"Hey, let's—," began Dave.

"No more hay!" yelled Allie, Amy, Marvin, and Gracie.

"I was just going to say we should go to the playground," said Dave.

The five gators raced there and burst through the gate.

"I'm going on the slide!" said Gracie.

"I'm going on the tire swing!" said Dave.

"Let's have a go on the whirl-a-round,"
said Alfie. "We can all go together."

...everyone ...got on and counted,
"One, two, three, go!"

The Gator Girls and Gator Boys kicked
off. The whirl-a-round started to spin.

"Faster! Faster!" ...said Amy and Allie.

And they tipped back their ... together as
they spun round and round and round...